Katie

THE REVOLTING
BRIDESMAID

Also available in the KATIE series

THE REVOLTING WEDDING

KATIE

THE REVOLTING
BRIDESMAID

MARY HOOPER

ILLUSTRATIONS BY
FREDERIQUE VAYSSIERE

BLOOMSBURY

Published in Great Britain in 2007 by Bloomsbury Publishing Plc
36 Soho Square, London, W1D 3QY

First published in the UK by Blackie Children's Books, 1990

A CIP catalogue record of this book is available from the
British Library

ISBN 978 0 7475 8611 1

Printed in Great Britain by Clays Ltd, St Ives Plc

1 3 5 7 9 10 8 6 4 2

All papers used by Bloomsbury Publishing are natural, recyclable products made
from wood grown in well-managed forests. The manufacturing processes conform to
the environmental regulations of the country of origin.

Typeset by Dorchester Typesetting Group Ltd

www.maryhooper.co.uk
www.bloomsbury.com/childrens

chapter one

I slid down the stairs and was about to do a forward roll into the sitting room when Mum ran into the hall and more or less threw herself across the door to stop me going in.

'Don't go in there now!' she said, waving her hands about and pulling a peculiar face. 'It's

Helen and Christopher!' And then she mouthed something excitedly and pulled me into the kitchen.

I looked at her in concern; she appeared to have gone quite loopy. 'Helen's doing what?' I asked.

'Sssh,' Mum said. 'She and Christopher are talking to Dad now. You know how he likes things to be done properly, your dad.'

'Helen and That Man,' I said in a louder voice, 'are doing *what*?'

'Sshh,' Mum said again, sitting down on the edge of the kitchen table. 'Getting married! People do, you know.'

'Not in this house they don't,' I said, amazed and a bit put out because I'd been the last to know something important again. 'Not often.'

'No, not often,' Mum said, 'just sometimes – and I do hope you're not going to be difficult, Katie. You must have seen the signs, after all.'

'What signs?'

'That she and Christopher were serious about each other, of course.'

Signs? I thought hard but couldn't remember seeing any. Real signs? Black and white HELEN

AND CHRISTOPHER ARE SERIOUS signs? I hadn't seen any of those.

Anyway, even if I had . . . I didn't exactly fancy the idea. OK, it would be nice to have Mum and Dad all to myself, but sometimes Helen could be fun. *And* she gave me her old make-up and clothes. Also, if she wasn't around I'd have to have old Mrs Crabbe down the road to babysit all the time. Besides, I certainly didn't want her to marry *him*. She'd been out with much nicer ones. He was too old for a start, and he wore old-fashioned trousers and stupid shirts patterned with little

cars or little trees. Worst of all, he was a teacher and kept asking me things about school in a bracing voice, like: 'How's the old history project going?' or, last week, on seeing me throwing my maths homework into the bin in disgust, 'In trouble with our binary numbers, are we?'

I tiptoed out of the kitchen and dropped on to all fours in front of the sitting-room door to try and listen to what was going on.

'Come away from that door at once!' Mum hissed from the kitchen. 'How's it going to look when they open it and you're kneeling there with

your ears flapping?'

'I'm not. I'm just sitting here examining the world of nature beneath the edge of this carpet,' I said. 'There's a little tiny thing with two hundred legs, a black beetle – well, half of one – a –'

'Come away from that door *now*!' Mum said sternly, but not before I heard him – That Man – saying something boring about mortgages and putting down deposits.

I reluctantly rolled over towards her and she looked at me and shook her head wearily. 'Now, before they come out, why don't you go upstairs and put on something other than that dreadful old tracksuit?'

'You bought this dreadful old tracksuit,' I pointed out. 'You wanted me to have one.'

'I didn't know you'd wear it day in and day out. It was clean when I bought it. Clean and pale pink,' she said with a sigh, 'and now it always seems to be grey.'

'She can't marry him!' I said urgently, ignoring the insults to my tracksuit. 'He's too old, for a start. He doesn't look like a bridegroom.'

'What do they look like, then?'

I thought back to a black and white film I'd seen on TV on Sunday afternoon. 'They're good-looking – like film stars – with slicked-back black hair and shiny shoes. They've got a bouquet of flowers in one hand and a diamond ring in a little box in the other.'

'I can't see any diamond rings forthcoming,' Mum said. 'Not on what he earns. And people don't have shiny shoes any more.'

'But he's old . . .' I wailed. 'Horribly old and fat.'

'Don't be silly,' Mum said. 'He's not at all fat. His face is chubby, that's all. And he's only twenty-nine.'

'That's what he tells you,' I said darkly.

'And Helen's twenty-two. That's a good age difference.'

'Fat, old and boring,' I said stubbornly. Of all the interesting people I could have had for a brother-in-law, I had to be lumbered with *him*.

'You'll not be losing a sister; you're gaining a brother,' Mum said.

'I don't want to gain a brother,' I said, infuriated. 'Not a brother like *him*, anyway. If she's got to

get married, then why can't it be someone in the royal family, or a pop star, or a DJ or someone exciting. Not him; *definitely* not him.'

'Well, I'm afraid it's not up to you,' she said. 'When you get married you're allowed to choose for yourself and I must say Dad and I are very –'

The sitting-room door handle rattled and Mum broke off and looked towards it expectantly, and then Helen and That Man came out holding hands and looking at each other with very silly grins.

'It's OK,' Helen said to Mum, smiling a big soppy smile. 'It's all arranged.'

'As if I actually had any say in the matter!' Dad shouted in a jolly voice, and then I heard glasses tinkling and he came through into the kitchen with a bottle of something on a tray.

I looked at That Man stonily: at his horrible shirt, silly trousers and face with a stupid pleased expression on it. The shame of it; imagine having to tell everyone that Helen was marrying *him*. I mean, couldn't she find anyone better? Surely she couldn't be that desperate?

I looked at Helen: she wasn't bad . . . she had frizzy red hair and lots of freckles and she dressed quite nicely . . . so was this frump in peculiar trousers honestly all she could get? But perhaps she hadn't looked properly; perhaps she needed a helping hand. Maybe it wasn't too late to find her someone better . . .

'Katie!' Mum said suddenly. 'How about having a little sip of something to celebrate?'

'And how about a kiss for your new brother?' That Man said heartily.

I screwed up my face in absolute disgust.

'Oh, Katie never kisses anyone,' Mum said hastily, moving to stand between him and my face.

'We've got another surprise for you!' Helen said, obviously not caring that she was leaning cosily against a shirt patterned with tiny fire engines. 'Something you've always wanted.'

'Not Disneyland?' I squealed. Maybe they were going there on honeymoon and taking me . . . if so, it wasn't too late for us to become instant best friends.

They laughed. 'Not quite that,' Helen said. 'The wedding will be quite soon – in September – and we want you to be our bridesmaid.'

'Yuk!' I said.

'Don't be silly, dear,' Mum said quickly and brightly. 'You've always wanted to be a bridesmaid.'

'That was when I was four!'

'Last year! You had a bride doll and you –'

'I never did!' I said hotly. 'Anyway, you bought it for me.'

'Well, anyway,' Helen said, 'Christopher and I would like you to be our bridesmaid and you'll

have a lovely dress and satin shoes and everything.'

I made an exaggerated sick noise and everyone
looked at me and tutted.

'At least it'll be interesting to see if she can be
prised out of that tracksuit,' Dad said.

'If you'll excuse me,' I said with dignity, 'I'm
going to my room to do homework. And yes, I am
getting on all right with my binary numbers,
thank you very much.' And I went off quickly
before anyone could shout at me.

I flung myself on my bed. The wedding was in
two months, but as it was the school holidays I
had plenty of free time to find Helen someone
better. My campaign would start immediately.

chapter two

'Isn't this all a bit sudden?' I said to Helen over breakfast the next morning. Mum and Dad had gone to work and I had to go to the Play Scheme with my friend Daisy later, but right then I had Helen all to myself and could begin the Campaign.

'What?' she said.

'This wedding and everything. I mean, you haven't known him long, have you?'

'For goodness' sake!' she said, sipping her coffee – she always has it black because she thinks it's sophisticated – 'What's it got to do with you?'

'A lot,' I said. 'If he's coming into the family I've got to approve of him, haven't I?'

'No, you haven't,' she said. 'And now you come to mention it I'd be very suspicious of anyone *you* approved of. Remember that park keeper you brought home who drank his way through all Dad's whisky before anyone could get rid of him? Remember the lady bus driver you invited along to your Macdonalds party?'

I looked at her darkly. 'Never mind them,' I said. 'I just want to remind you that the divorce rate is going up. You can't be too careful.'

'Oh, thanks a bundle,' she said. 'Here am I newly engaged and bursting with happiness and you're telling me about divorce rates.'

'I just want you to be sure,' I said in a goody-goody voice. 'Keira's sister only stayed with her new husband for three days after the honeymoon and Maria's mum and dad have just separated and Jess –'

'Spare me the details,' Helen said. 'I'll take my chances.'

'But is he all you could g—' I began, then amended it. 'But are you sure he's the Right One?' When I read the problem pages they were always talking about whether or not he was the Right One.

'You'd better let me worry about that, hadn't you?' she said. 'And I suggest you keep your cute little nose out of it and start growing your hair so

you'll make a pretty bridesmaid.'

I shuddered. 'I *like* my hair short in the summer. I had it cut extra short at the end of term specially – and I don't want to be a pretty bridesmaid, thank you.'

Helen swallowed the rest of her coffee and took her mug to the sink. 'Anyway,' she went on, 'since when have you started taking an interest in my boyfriends?'

'Since you started marrying them,' I said.

She groaned. 'Well, I'd really rather you left

them to me.' She fluffed her hair out in the mirror over the sink. 'It'll be quite nice for you, actually,' she said, 'because Christopher's going to be teaching at the new comprehensive – the one you'll be going to next September.'

I paused with a spoonful of cornflakes halfway to my mouth. 'Bradley Street?' I asked faintly.

'That's the one. He's going to be second-in-command in the English department. He can keep an eye on you . . . You can get bullied in big schools like that.'

I groaned . . . You can get bullied if your brother-in-law is a teacher, too – especially if he's a weirdo teacher with a silly fat baby face.

'Is the job definite?' I asked carefully.

'Oh yes!' she said. 'He had the letter last week. That's what made us decide to get married – he'll be earning more money, you see.'

'Fancy,' I said, lowering the spoon. I wasn't hungry. Things were more awful than I'd thought.

'Now,' Helen said, 'Christopher's parents are coming over tonight and I want you to be on your best behaviour.' She looked me up and down. 'You can get out of that tracksuit – that's if it actually comes off – get Mum to do something about your hair, and do make sure you answer politely when they ask about things – oh, and tidy your room.'

'They're not going to look in my room!'

'They might . . . they might want to look over the house.'

'Why do I have to see them anyway?' I muttered.

'Because they want to meet *you*.' She looked at me and rolled her eyes. 'I know that sounds unlikely but they want to see the size of you to compare you with Christopher's cousin.'

I looked at her, bewildered. 'What for?'

'Because she's the other bridesmaid, of course. I told you last night.'

'I don't remember.'

'No. You were too busy glowering at Christopher.' She suddenly sat down again and put her arm round me. 'There's no need to be jealous, you know, Katie. I'm not going to go far. We'll still be sisters.'

'I'm not jealous!' I said, shrugging the arm off indignantly. 'I don't care if you're getting married!' I just don't want you to marry someone who's old and boring and who's going to be an embarrassment to me, I thought.

'Well, OK, then,' she said, miffed. 'So you will tidy your room, won't you? And get out of that tracksuit by tonight? And help us tidy the house? And be on your very best behaviour – which means not rolling about the floor doing gymnastics.'

'Anything else?' I asked. 'Perhaps you'd like me to enrol for a Charm School course, too.'

'In your case that might be a very good idea,' she said, and she went out humming something that sounded suspiciously like the 'Wedding March'.

A bit later Mum rang.

'Now, darling, I'll be home from work early but I want you to push the vacuum cleaner round the house – just to give me a start,' she said. 'Christopher's parents are visiting tonight and I want everything –'

'I know,' I interrupted.

'And make sure your blue dress is clean. And if you could pop down to the shop for me and . . .'

I left the receiver dangling and went to get some writing paper. Sitting on the stairs I could still hear, 'And if you get a moment could you . . . Oh! and also would you . . .' as I began my letter.

Things were deadly serious. Desperate measures were called for. Surely someone could help me get her a boyfriend . . .

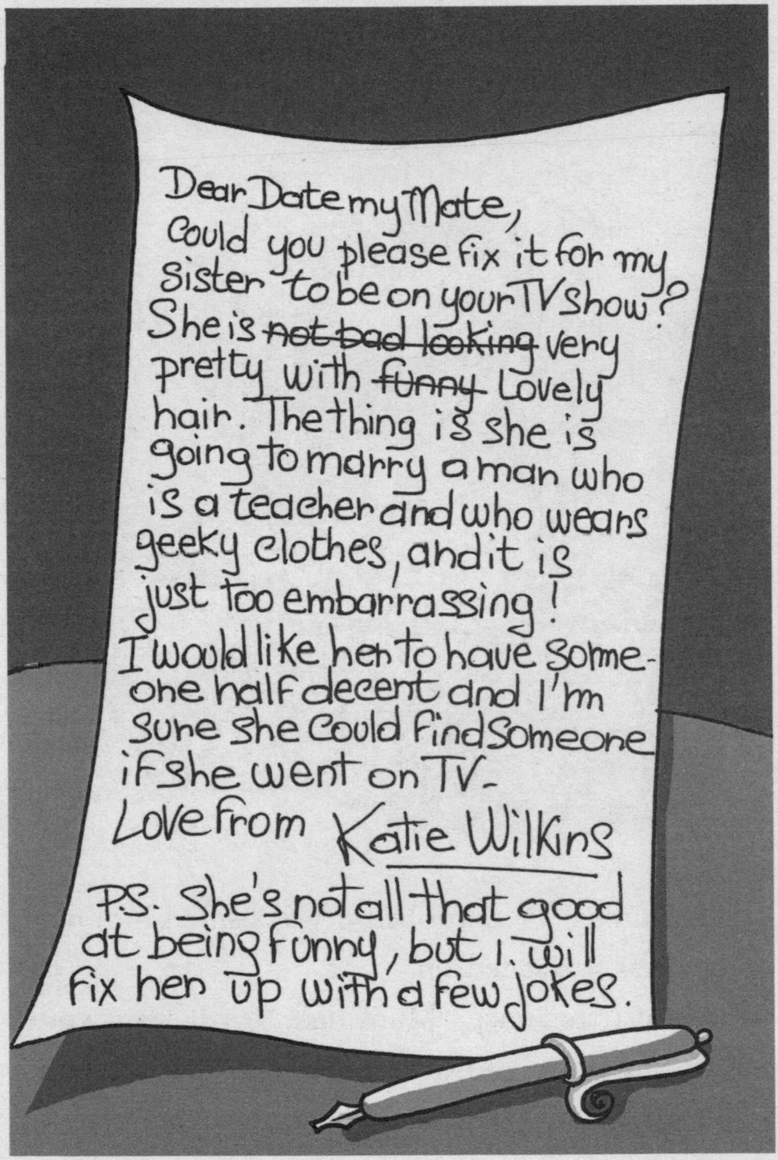
Dear Date my Mate,
Could you please fix it for my sister to be on your TV show?
She is ~~not bad looking~~ very pretty with ~~funny~~ Lovely hair. The thing is she is going to marry a man who is a teacher and who wears geeky clothes, and it is just too embarrassing!
I would like her to have someone half decent and I'm sure she could find someone if she went on TV.
Love from Katie Wilkins
P.S. She's not all that good at being funny, but I will fix her up with a few jokes.

chapter three

I was shiny. I was scrubbed. I was stuffed into my blue dress. I was fed up.

'It's just this once,' Mum lied. 'I just want you to sit quietly in the sitting room with a book on your knee. You can change back into your tracksuit when they've gone.'

'Mum,' I said plaintively, 'it's far better that they see me as I really am.'

Something like a shudder ran across her face. 'Not just at the moment, Katie, because we want them to have a good first impression of us and that might be difficult with you wearing a washed out grey thing with smelly trainers on your feet with one toe sticking out.' She paused and looked at me, head on one side. 'I wish we hadn't had your hair cut quite so short, but it looks almost pretty when it's brushed – I'd practically forgotten. Mrs Bailey will be looking at your hairstyle, you see, and trying to think what sort of a head-dress would suit you.'

'She's not choosing everything!'

'Well . . .' Mum said delicately, 'Mrs Bailey is the After Six Cocktail and Continental Cruise Wear Buyer in Bliss's Store, you see, so she wants to be in charge of the bridal party.'

'Well, Mrs Bayleaf isn't going to be in charge of me!' I said heatedly. Anyway, with a bit of luck, *Date My Mate* permitting, there wasn't going to be any wedding. I hoped they wrote back quickly . . . I could do with Helen being on the programme immediately – before this Mrs Bayleaf person started ordering me into something with ten metres of sequins sewn all over it.

'We thought a big crinoline dress for you,' Mum said. 'Pale green with ra-ra frills in lace all the way down and six big red bows over the front.'

I sprang up out of the chair and the book fell on to the floor. 'Never!' I said. 'I'd rather die than wear anything like that. I'll run away . . . join an orphanage . . .'

But Mum was laughing. 'Don't be silly,' she said. 'It won't be anything like that. We'll get a lovely dress that you'll enjoy wearing.'

'I won't,' I said, 'unless it's going to be grey and snuggly like my tracksuit.'

'Now,' Mum said, 'do sit down again and try to look quiet and tidy – that means no rolling round the floor.' She disappeared, tutting steadily, to rearrange a vase of flowers that wasn't quite to her liking.

Elsewhere in the house I could hear noises that meant we were about to be descended on by the Bayleaves. In the bathroom Dad was gargling – he smoked a pipe and always gargled before anyone

important came in case he breathed tobacco breath on them – and Helen was dashing up and down the stairs saying things like, 'Five minutes . . . I'll never be ready . . . The place is like a tip . . . I forgot to get the fresh coffee . . . Why aren't there any flowers in the hall? . . . I can't bear it . . . I know you won't get on . . . It's all going to be horrendous . . .'

My friend Daisy hadn't been a lot of help. *Her* sister had got married two years ago and apparently Daisy had enjoyed every minute of it.

'Everyone makes a fuss of you and says how lovely you are and you get in hundreds of photographs,' she said wistfully. 'And the bride throws the bouquet and you catch it and then everyone says you'll get married next, and then the best man dances with you and you get a little bit of cake in a box and a present from the bridegroom.'

'Yuk, yuk and more yuk.'

Every time she said anything I groaned a bit more. I didn't want a rotten silk dress with rotten satin shoes *or* a bit of cake in a box. 'What's the present?' I asked.

'A silver cross and chain,' she said. 'But the

chain makes your neck go black.'

'Great,' I said sourly. 'What's he like though –
your bridegroom?'

'Ooh, he's lovely,' she said. 'He works for a firm
that makes sweets and gives me loads of chocolate.
Every Easter he brings me home all the broken
Easter eggs. Sometimes they're just things like
chocolate rabbits with a couple of ears missing.'

I sighed. Nothing could be more wonderful
than to have someone in the family who brought
home chocolate, broken or otherwise. *I* was having
someone who brought home binary numbers.

There was a ring on the doorbell and I felt the whole house pause for a moment, rigid with horror, and then redouble their efforts at everything: Dad gargled twice as fast, Helen ran up and down the stairs at the speed of sound and Mum, returning with the flowers (which didn't look any different), paused in the doorway and took little quick dance steps backwards and forwards, not sure whether to put the flowers down, go to the door or what.

'I'll go, shall I?' I said.

'No! No, Helen should go!' Mum said, and then called in a voice that was half a whisper and half a scream: 'Helen! Door!'

'I heard it!' Helen said in the same anguished screamy voice and then she came down, saying in a harsh undertone to Mum, 'Pick that up! Why is that there? The hall light's too dim! Is the coffee on?' and then she opened the door and her voice immediately changed to become all dripping with smarm. 'Good evening, Mrs Bailey . . . Mr Bailey. Lovely to see you!' And then to That Man, 'Hello, *darling*!'

I sat rigid in my allotted chair, eyes glued to the

book as I'd been instructed. My campaign tonight would mostly consist of just surveying the Bayleaves and working out the best plan for breaking up this unsuitable relationship. Of course, if they happened to find me a little odd, all the better. Maybe it would make them consider the wisdom of mingling with our family on a permanent in-laws type basis . . .

chapter four

'And this is our younger daughter, Katie,' Mum said as Mr and Mrs Bayleaf paused in front of my chair.

'How do you *do*, dear?' Mrs Bayleaf said smarmily, and I looked up from my book, surprised, as if I'd only just noticed that someone had come into the room. I blinked at her as if she was a strange creature from outer space – and she did look rather strange, actually, being a huge woman wearing a frilled nylon dress, crossed over and pinned in the front with a sparkly brooch in the shape of a spider. The dress was vast and billowy and printed with all manner of green plant-like shapes so that the whole effect was of a small walking greenhouse.

She smiled down at me, her face pink and fat and well powdered, her eyes sparkling.

'Mrs Bailey's got some lovely ideas for bridesmaids' dresses,' Mum said, hoping to stir me into some comment by poking my foot with the tip of her toe.

'And Mr Bailey just thinks he'll emigrate until September's over,' Mr Bayleaf said, settling down in the sofa next to Dad.

'How interesting,' I said to Mum. 'And now I really must get back to my book.'

'What is it, dear?' asked Mrs Bayleaf.

'*British Birds and Their Mating Habits*,' I said.

Mum poked me harder. 'I'm sure it's not that – not mating habits,' she said. 'It's just Katie's idea of a joke.'

I looked at her wide-eyed, demure. 'It is,' I said. 'It's got some very interesting bits here about the wag-tailed Pyewacket. Did you know that when it wants to mate it goes to the top of a tree and –'

'Do sit down, Mrs Bailey!' Mum interrupted.

'Beattie, dear. Beattie,' Mrs Bayleaf said. 'If we're going to be family we ought to be Beattie and Cedric to you.'

'Of course,' Mum said. 'And we're Sally and Richard.'

Everyone settled down uneasily and began talking about the weather and other riveting topics. Mum occasionally directed a question at me, but when she did I just frowned slightly at being disturbed from my book. Good and quiet, she'd said; don't move, she'd said. The two 'love-birds' as Mrs Bayleaf called them, started compiling a guest list for the wedding.

'Everyone for coffee?' Mum asked after about half an hour, and then there was a long and tedious roll call during which people decided

whether they wanted it black or white – cream or milk. And sugared or non-sugared – sweeteners or brown sugar.

'Perhaps you could come and help me, Katie,' Mum said pointedly, and I had to go into the kitchen with her.

'Why are you sitting there like a dummy?' she hissed when we were on our own. 'Mrs Bailey will think you can't speak.'

'You said to be quiet and good,' I said. 'I'm just following instructions.'

'I didn't say you had to sit there like a stuffed prune. At least try and let her see you're alive.'

I shook my head helplessly. 'I was only following instructions,' I said. '*You* said I was to just sit there with a book and be quiet and –'

'Will you stop saying that and take this coffee pot in immediately,' Mum said grimly. 'Furthermore, you're given permission to stop reading so that you can make polite conversation with Mrs Bailey.'

'And is the little princess looking forward to being a bridesmaid?' Mrs Bayleaf trilled at me when I put the coffee pot down.

'Not really,' I said politely. 'I don't like dressing
up. I particularly don't like frilly dresses or things
with bows.'

'Ah, weddings are different, though,' she said.
'Weddings are the one time we can let our hair
down and indulge.'

I stared at her, resplendent in a whole forest of
greens. It looked like she'd indulged already.

'Now, your little counterpart – Felicity – has
already started talking about what colour she
wants. A delightful child Felicity is, simply
delightful.' I stared at her stonily, hating Felicity

quietly and desperately. 'She's got lovely golden curls,' – here Mrs Bayleaf looked at my short stubby hair and shook her head sadly – 'so we thought pale lemon would look fabbo. Something in watered silk, perhaps, with just the weeniest little peplum frill round the middle and the tiniest indulgence of embroidered flowers across the bosom.'

'How gorgeous!' Mum said, coming back in with the home-made biscuits and looking at me pointedly. 'Doesn't that sound lovely, Katie?'

I didn't say anything.

'Speak up, darling,' Mum said, a note of desperation in her voice.

'I can't,' I said. 'You told me I had to be polite.'

'Ha ha!' Mum laughed falsely. 'Don't they show you up, these children!'

Mrs Bayleaf's powdered face creased and smirked at me. She obviously thought I was quite overcome with awe at the thought of such a dress. 'And I thought the sweetest little circlet of artificial flowers around the head . . .' she went on, 'with perhaps a dinky artificial pearl dropping gracefully over the forehead.'

'Will you excuse me?' I said earnestly and politely. 'I have to go to the lavatory.'

chapter five

It was a few days later when Helen pushed me through the front door and prodded me all the way down the hall into the kitchen where Mum was peeling potatoes.

'I've never been so humiliated in my life,' she said dramatically. 'Never!'

She put down the bags she was carrying on the kitchen table and flopped on to a chair. 'It's been a nightmare, an absolute nightmare!'

Mum looked directly at me with an exasperated expression. 'Whatever's she done now?' she said.

'Why d'you look straight at me?' I said indignantly. 'How d'you know I've got anything to do with it?'

'Sixth sense,' Mum said, just as Helen burst out with another chorus of 'Dreadful . . . I'll never get over the embarrassment . . . So humiliating . . . I just can't tell you,' following which she managed to tell us without drawing breath.

'We met Mrs Bailey in Country Casuals and Tweeds as arranged,' she started, and as she spoke I slid sideways towards the door. I'd noticed a typed letter addressed to me on the hall table and I was desperate to get to it.

'Get back here!' Helen said. 'I want you to hear what Mum's got to say about all this.'

'There's a letter for me . . .' I muttered.

'Here!' Helen said, just as if I was a dog.

I sat down at the table and waited for the storm to break over me.

'As I said,' Helen started again, 'we met Mrs Bailey and she took us along to The Brides' Bouquet –'

'I don't know why it's called the Brides' Bouquet,' I interrupted, playing for time. 'It's a silly name, isn't it, Mum? It's not a bunch of flowers. Why don't they call it the Brides' Boudoir or the Brides' –'

'Why don't you shut up?' Helen said fiercely.

'Or the Brides' Business,' I said quietly.

'We started looking through wedding dresses. I quite liked the look of ivory but Mrs Bailey said very pale pink was fashionable this year.'

'Or Brides' Boutique . . .' I said in a whisper.

'Well, I hadn't actually tried anything on – I still couldn't decide on the shade – and we were about to move on to bridesmaids' dresses to keep *her* here amused, but when I looked round for her she'd gone. Disappeared.'

Mum tutted. 'She's always wandering off. Fancy disappearing when you're supposed to be looking at bridesmaids' dresses, though, Katie!'

'Oh, she hadn't *disappeared*,' Helen said heavily and sarcastically. 'I wouldn't have minded if she'd disappeared, I would have quite liked that. Oh no, what she'd *done* was pick up some awful macho yob . . . and try to get us together.'

'What?' Mum asked faintly.

'It's perfectly true, I promise you,' Helen said. 'I've never been so humiliated in my life. Never. There I was actually *choosing* my wedding dress and I turned round and there she was with some awful lout in tow saying, "Helen, someone wants to meet you." I don't know *what* Mrs Bailey must think of us, I really don't. I could just die of humiliation every time I think of it.'

I tried to make myself invisible by leaning back hard against the wall but I don't think it worked. Two pairs of eyes bored into me accusingly.

'Katie!' Mum said. 'How could you?'

'I was just trying to be helpful,' I said. 'Just trying to give Helen the opportunity of . . . of meeting other men before it's too late. I was trying to save the divorce rate. Besides, Mrs Bayleaf didn't even notice – she was too busy flaunting herself round the department and bossing people about.'

They carried on staring at me, anguish and

horror written all over their faces.

'He was dead cool,' I blustered, 'like he was in a boy band or something. He was the sort of person a girl wouldn't *mind* having for a brother-in-law.'

'He was dreadful,' Helen said faintly. 'He was wearing a disgusting-looking hoody and jeans that hung down so far they showed his pants. He had a piercing through his eyebrow, for goodness' sake! And apart from anything else he was about ten years younger than me.'

'That's because you're used to old men,' I said. 'He had a really cool pair of trainers . . .'

'*Katie!*' Mum said again, and it seemed to me

that people were saying my name like that all the time lately – in an anguished voice with an exclamation mark at the end.

I felt Mum and Helen exchange head shakes and eye-rollings while I pretended an intense interest in the pattern of the tablecloth.

'Katie, haven't you always been told never to speak to strangers?' Mum said. 'And how *could* you embarrass your sister like that?'

'Didn't seem any harm in it,' I mumbled. 'He was just hanging about outside the Brides' Whatsit –'

'Probably a shoplifter,' Helen said.

'– and he looked really nice so I said would he like to come with me and meet my sister. OK, so you didn't want to meet him but I wasn't to know that, was I? I just thought you might like to meet someone really interesting and cool instead of a –'

'Katie!' Mum said warningly. 'That's quite enough. I think you'd better go upstairs now and just think about what you've done.'

'Right!' I said, moving to the door in a trice.

'Do you know, I've a good mind not to let you be a bridesmaid!' Helen said, but before I could get too excited she added, 'If it wasn't for having you to match Felicity I'd just do without you.'

As I went down the hall I heard them falling on the bags of bits and pieces Helen had bought and exclaiming over them excitedly — so much for Helen's total and utter humiliation which would stay with her for ever. I snatched up my letter from the table and ran upstairs with it. OK, so one of my plans had failed but this letter could be the answer to everything.

Dear Katie Wilkins,

Thank you for your letter but we are sorry to have to tell you that the new series of Date My Mate *has already been filmed and we will not be needing any more contestants for another year.*

Perhaps you should also know that we receive hundreds of applications from people who actually want to take part so never have to resort to using people who've been nominated for the show by their relatives!

We hope your sister will be very happy in her forthcoming marriage and that you have a lovely day.

Yours sincerely,

Researcher

I screwed the letter up into a little ball and threw it away. What a waste of a stamp. I would have to think of something else . . .

chapter six

I picked at the balls of fluff that for some reason had congregated along the sleeve of my tracksuit and stared moodily out of my bedroom window. I was fed up. I was getting nowhere with the Campaign and every day the wedding was coming closer.

'I bet it's getting really exciting in your house, isn't it?' Daisy had said that morning.

'Oh yes,' I'd said gloomily. 'Really exciting.'

'Are they having a present display?' she asked. 'My sister had a big table in the spare room and after the wedding all the guests walked by it and admired what they'd bought.'

'Dunno,' I said. 'I think it's a cheek, anyway. Fancy sending out *lists* of things they want.'

'That's so they don't get six toasters,' she said wisely. 'But then some people don't ask for the list so it goes wrong anyway. My sister still got five toasters,' she added.

'I'm going to make a list next birthday and send it out,' I said. 'See how people like that.'

'Has your sister got The Dress yet?' Daisy asked in a hushed and excited voice.

'Dunno,' I said again. 'No one tells me anything and I'm not even allowed to go shopping with them now. Something as big as an elephant arrived wrapped in a big sheet the other day; I suppose that was it.'

'And what about *your* dress?'

'Whisper blue with taffeta overskirt, exquisite

49

beaded bodice and puff sleeves,' I reeled off automatically. 'It's being let out and I've got another fitting for it next week. The darling little circlet of flowers are being made fresh on the day,' I added, and then made a face which meant I was likely to be sick.

Daisy went into fresh squeals of excitement at this and I gave her a withering look to get her to shut up. I soon made it up with her, though. I find I often do when people have got a lot of chocolate in their pockets.

If only he, That Man, worked for a chocolate firm. Or was anything, in fact, except a teacher. The previous evening he'd wanted to sit down with me – in the school holidays, mind – and go over all I could remember about dividing sentences into their correct grammatical parts. I said I couldn't remember anything, upon which he got so concerned and upset that I thought he was going to cry. He said I really ought to be up on them before next year so how about sitting down for half an hour so he could help me? It was then that I decided it was time for an early night.

I sighed, finished picking at my sleeve and then

sat down and thumbed through one of Mum's magazines. I came to the problem page and thought about writing to it for advice on getting rid of That Man, but then a bit further on I found an advertisement by a firm called Superdate which sounded *just* what I was looking for.

SOMEONE FOR EVERYONE!

No one should settle for second best when they could meet the Person of Their Dreams! Girls — meet Prince Charming! Boys — meet Cinderella!

Yes! You too could be the Happiest Person in the

World when you meet that SUPERDATE personally handpicked and supplied by us.

Money back guarantee! Golden opportunity of a lifetime! Put a lotta cuddles in your life!

No one should settle for second best! I thought, filling in the form with Helen's details and naturally exaggerating her characteristics to give her more of a chance. For ginger hair I put 'gorgeous auburn' and when it said, *Give yourself an attractiveness rating of 1 to 10*, I put 20 with a load of exclamation marks behind it. The thing was, when I got down to the end of the form it said in very small print: *Give us your credit card number and we will debit your account for £50.*

I crumpled up the form. I didn't have a credit card and I didn't think Helen would let me use hers – especially if she knew what I wanted it for.

As I was crumpling I had a brilliant idea, though. All the Superdate place was doing, really, was advertising people – so why couldn't I do that myself and save money? Why not, in other words, put my own advert for Helen on the local newsagent's board with the cars and flats and second-hand sofas? OK, so it wouldn't reach as big a market as Superdate, but finding someone who lived locally would be so much more convenient.

I carefully wrote a few of Helen's vital statistics on a postcard – there wasn't a lot of room so I just put something about a gorgeous redhead seeking a new friend – and took the card down to the shop on the corner.

I felt extremely pleased with myself as I walked home: I'd more or less done the same thing as Superdate, but I'd saved £49.75! It would be quite interesting, too: they could phone up, I'd

interview them and then invite them round to meet Helen. She needn't know where they'd come from, I'd just line up all the best ones on the settee ready for her inspection.

I still felt extremely pleased with myself at tea time, but at about five-thirty when I answered the phone and someone just breathed down it I started to have second and then third thoughts.

'Huff . . . Huff . . . Huff . . .' someone said breathily, and I listened, panicked, slammed the phone down and rushed to the newsagent's to get the notice taken out of the window. Not one of my better ideas.

I'd obviously have to think of something else.

chapter seven

'Do try and stand still, dear,' Mrs Bayleaf said, giving one of her royal family smiles and displaying a great swatch of gold fillings.

'Katie! For goodness' sake stop wriggling!' Mum snapped. She rolled her eyes. 'I'm sorry, Mrs Bailey. She's not usually such a pain.'

We were in Bliss's Bridal Bouquet fitting room where I'd been forced into my whisper blue dress with taffeta overskirt, exquisite beaded bodice and puff sleeves.

'There's things sticking in me,' I complained, frowning down at the alterations lady who was deliberately making me suffer. 'And a bit of exquisite beading has come off and fallen down my neck.'

Mum sighed. 'The lady's nearly finished, Katie. Just stand still and be patient a while longer.'

After what seemed like about six hours the alteration lady stood up and said she was almost satisfied. 'I'm just going to let the bodice out the tiniest bit more,' she said. 'Other than that our young lady looks perfect.'

I glowered at myself in the mirror: I didn't look at all perfect to me – more like a dog's dinner. From the neck down I was a froth of whisper blue, but out of this stuck an indignant-looking face topped by stubbly hair sticking out all over the place. I looked like part of one of those card games where you fit different heads on bodies and make strange combinations.

'A vision of loveliness . . .' Mrs Bayleaf pronounced. 'Almost, that is. We've just got to do something about that hair.'

'Yes, you look lovely, darling,' Mum said uncertainly. 'Very . . . er . . . different.'

'Can I take if off now?' I asked plaintively, but they'd started a conversation about veils – should or shouldn't Helen have one over her face as she went into the church? – and had forgotten about me, so I took the dress off anyway and climbed back into my tracksuit and trainers.

We went into the shoe section next door to collect my satin ballet shoes which had not only been dyed to match, but also had some exquisite beading on them. I couldn't see why because the dress would cover them up, but still – what Mrs Bayleaf wanted Mrs Bayleaf got. What she didn't know about well-dressed weddings wasn't worth knowing.

While we were waiting for the shoes to be wrapped in tissue, Mrs Bayleaf got out some photographs of Felicity, whose dress was being fitted at the Bliss's store near where she lived.

'I thought it would be nice for you to see what little Felicity is like,' Mrs Bayleaf said. 'She's a little slimmer than you . . .' – she looked thoughtfully at my midriff, inflated lately by Daisy's chocolate pieces – '. . . but do you know, she's exactly the same height as you. Isn't that lucky?'

While Mum marvelled over this amazing piece of good luck I looked at the photographs and groaned quietly to myself. She was just how I'd expected her to be: thin and pale and blonde, with luxuriant hair that hung to her shoulders in perfect curls. She also had a simpering goody-goody

expression on her face.

'You can imagine how the flower circlet will look on *that* hair,' Mrs Bayleaf said with a soft smile.

I didn't trust myself to speak. I felt positively ill at the thought of the wedding day when I'd be stuck with this simpering blonde thing. Of course, she'd be the absolutely perfect bridesmaid and for ever after I'd be compared to her and found lacking in all the bridesmaidly qualities. Wasn't Felicity a perfect bridesmaid? they'd say. Wasn't Felicity the most wonderful bridesmaid the world had ever seen? All the more reason for getting rid of That Man. Get rid of him and Felicity would go, too.

We collected the shoes and Mrs Bayleaf escorted us to the store exit. 'Now, my dear, everything's in order, isn't it?' she said to Mum. She ticked things off on her fingers: 'The wedding dress has arrived . . . the headdress . . . the shoes . . . the veil.' She bent over Mum and kissed the air at the side of her cheek. 'It's such a relief! I'm so pleased my son is marrying your Helen!' she gushed, which immediately gave me a brilliant idea. Instead of trying to turn Helen off him, why didn't I try a completely new angle and try to turn *him* off *her*? It was worth a try, anyway. Anything was worth a try at this stage to prevent me being the laughing stock of the entire school.

I thought about it all the way home and started as soon as we got in. Helen and That Man were installed in the kitchen having coffee and he proved what a crawler he was by immediately jumping up, giving Mum his seat and pouring her out a coffee from the jug.

Helen moved towards me to take my bag and

see what we'd bought and I flinched away from her nervously.

'No, don't hit me!' I said in a wonderfully frightened voice. 'Please don't hit me again!'

She looked at me, astonished. 'Why on earth should I hit you? What have you done?'

I managed a very authentic-looking shiver. 'I don't always have to have *done* anything for you to hit me, do I?'

That Man looked round in astonishment and Helen, taken aback, goggled at me. 'What on earth are you talking about?'

'You know . . .' I said darkly, and I moved very stealthily round the kitchen to get some orange out of the fridge, pressing myself against the walls and trying to keep out of her reach.

'Don't be so silly, Katie,' Mum said briskly. 'What do you think you're up to now?'

'You might not know everything that goes on in his house,' I said mysteriously, looking at Helen as if she might spring at me at any moment.

Mum shook her head slowly and thoughtfully. 'I sometimes wonder about you, Katie, I really do,' she said in a resigned voice. 'Perhaps it's too much television or something.'

'Can . . . can I go to my room?' I asked in a terrified whisper.

'Yes, for goodness' sake do!' Mum said, and I slunk out of the room and ran upstairs. *That* would make him have second thoughts all right.

chapter eight

It didn't, though. I managed a couple of days slinking around the house like an injured dog and giving plaintive whimpers whenever Helen came near me, but no one took any notice. In fact, in the end they started treating it as a big joke and all had a good laugh about it. So I abandoned that plan and started thinking about others.

It was all getting a bit close, though. Presents had started arriving: presents in lovely big colourful boxes with silver ribbon and bows. I felt quite sick with jealousy until they were opened and I saw the sort of things that were inside: boring things like steam irons, wine glasses, matching his 'n' hers bath robes, pillow cases and enough tea-towels for each day of the year. No toasters so far.

One afternoon Mum sent me up to Helen's bedroom to leave some brochures for a car hire company on her desk. I put them down and then

I sat on her bed looking round, thinking deeply. Above the desk were two pinboards stuck all over with old photographs – pre-That Man photographs – and I crossed to have a look at them. They were mostly holiday snaps: Helen and me in the sea in Cornwall, Helen building a sand-castle for me at Brighton, Helen taking me on the ghost train at Blackpool. One *really* interested me, though: Helen and a holiday romance of hers in Newquay.

I thought back . . . it had been three years ago when I'd been about seven. He – the holiday

romance — had been staying at the same boarding house as us and I hadn't really noticed him until suddenly Helen wasn't available to look after me or take me to the amusement park, Helen was only to be seen walking off into the distance with her arms round . . . I thought hard . . . Michael or Mick or . . . or *Mark* — that was his name.

There were several photographs of him and he'd really been quite reasonable now I looked at him closely: certainly better than a tiresome teacher in peculiar trousers.

What had happened to him, though? As far as I could remember she hadn't seen him any more after the holiday . . . but I could vaguely remember seeing her mooning about the house waiting for letters, looking out of the window for the postman and sighing a lot. I could also remember being sent out of the room so she could have earnest discussions with Mum.

Great! I sprang back from the pinboard on to the bed and then did a forward flip off it. It wasn't too late! Memories of the holiday romance could be revived and Helen, when she thought about Mark again and all the good times they'd had, would suddenly realise that he had been the Real Thing and that That Man was completely wrong for her.

I somersaulted back to my own room. There wasn't time for 'Helen' – in other words, me – to write to Mark, having suddenly discovered that she still loved him, and she wouldn't be fooled for a minute if I made up a letter and pretended it had come from him. No, it had to be cleverer than that, cleverer and quicker.

I stared out of my window into the front garden waiting for inspiration to strike, and it did, almost immediately. Flowers! Of course; the very thing. Flowers from Mark to Helen with all his love, saying he'd never forgotten the holiday and was still pining for her. Perhaps there could be a PS saying that he was sorry he hadn't written but his arm had been broken until quite recently. OK, I reasoned, thinking of possible objections to this story – it seemed a bit far-fetched but what if it had been a particularly bad break . . . in both arms . . . and they'd been set wrongly and had to be re-broken several times and started again?

I wandered down to the garden and studied the

flowers. Dad and Mum hate gardening so there wasn't much: half a dozen dahlias and some dead-looking daisies that smelt awful. Helen obviously wasn't going to get swept off her feet and cancel the wedding because of *those*. No, if I was going to do it I had to do it properly: a bouquet in cellophane delivered by a proper florist with card and everything. It would cost me, but if it did the trick it would be worth every penny.

At six o'clock that evening – the time I'd given the florist to deliver the flowers – everything went perfectly. Helen had just come in from work and was in the hall fiddling about with her hair – she'd been trying out different hairstyles to see which would look better under the tiara Mrs Bayleaf had recommended – and I was sitting hidden at the top of the stairs watching.

The doorbell rang, the flowers arrived, Helen gave a little shriek of excitement and, putting the flowers down on the hall table, ripped the card off the top. Now, I'd been very clever here: instead of putting a long excuse and explanation (and besides, there wasn't room on the card) I'd just put 'For ever . . . M.' This, I thought, was far more

exciting and mysterious. It wouldn't take her long to work out who 'M' was – especially if gently reminded by me.

So far so good. I peered over the top and watched her face as she read the card. 'For ever . . . M.' I heard her mutter in a puzzled voice, and then her face cleared as if she'd realised – just as the doorbell rang and That Man arrived.

Now, I thought, now there would be ructions and rows. He'd be wildly jealous and she'd say it was just a very old friend and then he'd throw the flowers on the floor and stamp on them and she'd say what a disgusting display of temper and he was to leave the house immediately.

But Helen threw her arms round his neck.

'Darling!' she said. 'Darling Mousey-wouse!'

'Wh . . . what?' he said.

'These flowers! Oh Mouse! How romantic. You're just the darlingest Mouse in the world to go to a florists and send me flowers. I suppose you were too embarrassed to put "from Mouse".'

'Helen, I . . .' he started again, but she was making silly squeaky mouse noises in his ear. He tried once more and then I saw him shrug slightly, as if he'd decided that it didn't matter if she didn't believe him and he might as well take the credit for them anyway.

They went into the kitchen together, arms round each other and both making silly squeaky noises. I sat gloomily at the top of the stairs, thought about how much the flowers had cost and wondered about rolling down the stairs and breaking a couple of legs so they'd have to cancel the wedding.

chapter nine

'Helen?' I said in a strange squeaky voice down the phone. 'No, there's no one of that name living here. Helen who?'

'Helen Wilkins,' That Man said wearily, 'and I know it's you, Katie.'

'Katie? Who's Katie? There's no one of that

name living here,' I said, pushing my big toe as far as possible through the hole in my trainers and wriggling it. 'Please replace the receiver and try again.'

'No, I will *not* replace the receiver, Katie,' he suddenly said in a bossy, schoolmasterly voice, 'so please go and get Helen this instant.'

'She's out,' I said sulkily.

'Out? Where out?'

'I don't know,' I said. 'She doesn't tell me everything. A big car arrived for her and she went off with a strange man and . . . oops!' I cried falsely, 'I wasn't supposed to say anything.'

'Katie!' Helen came running down the stairs. 'Is that for me? What are you doing? Why didn't you call me?'

She snatched the phone out of my hand and I looked at her in pretend surprise. 'Oh, you're back! I didn't realise.'

'Stupid! I've never been out!' she hissed, and then she turned her back on me and said, '*Darling*!' followed by some squeaky mouse noises.

I pushed my big toe back in and went into the kitchen. Behind me I heard, 'No, I'm sure she's

not all there lately. She does the strangest things
... mmm ... makes up stories ... Yes, quite,
quite loopy ... Perhaps it's her age ... No, of
course I wasn't like it, darling.'

In the kitchen, Mum was standing knee-deep in
tissue paper and cardboard box. An enormous
white three-tiered cake – the wedding cake – sat
on the kitchen table. I ignored it.

'Anything to eat?' I said. 'I'm starving to death.'

'What do you think about this gorgeous
creation?' Mum asked. 'I just had to assemble it to

see what it looked like. Now, do you think this little bride and groom look best on top . . .' she sat them on with a flourish, 'or . . .' she whisked them off and put on a silver vase of dried flowers, 'this flower arrangement done by Mrs Bailey?'

'The bride and groom,' I said. 'Anything to eat?'

Mum gestured round the kitchen. 'Find yourself something, can you?'

I looked round. The worktops were covered thickly with little pastry objects: round things, triangular puff things, sausage rolls and bits-on-sticks. On the window sill sat a vast turkey, on the

washing machine was a joint of meat about as big as an elephant and on the fridge was what looked like a small whale. I approached the small whale and, taking a knife from the kitchen drawer, started hacking a piece off.

Mum gave a horrified scream. 'The salmon! Don't touch my beautiful poached salmon! It's going next door to Mrs Roger's fridge.' She turned back to the wedding cake. 'I'm not perfectly happy with the bride and groom . . .' she said to herself. 'The bride has such a funny expression on her face. I rather wonder if the flower arrangement . . .'

'I'll have these, then,' I said, getting a plate and collecting myself half a dozen little pastry things.

'Not the vol-au-vents!' she cried in anguish, seeming to have eyes in the back of her head. 'There are only a hundred prawn ones!'

'I'll just starve then, shall I?'

'Do you think this little bride is cross-eyed?' Mum asked thoughtfully. 'And isn't her mouth a bit twisted?'

I stood near the turkey and, pretending to be fascinated by the drama being played out on the wedding cake, managed to pull off a lump of crispy skin and a chunk of flesh.

This was what it had come to: I was reduced to foraging for food in my own house. Things were impossible; everything in the world moved around The Wedding. Things were delivered at all hours, vicars called, Mrs Bayleaf loomed out of the night with boxes, brochures were pored over, people were continually on the phone saying, 'But we *must* have it for Saturday! It's absolutely imperative that we have it then.' If I moved out I didn't think anyone would notice – apart from being pleased to have the extra space.

Earlier that day a present had arrived in the mail van from Felicity: 'To the happy couple from your bridesmaid' it said, and when it was unwrapped from its box of wood shavings it turned out to be a thin crystal vase, the most beautiful vase anyone had ever seen, such taste, such delicacy, how terribly thoughtful of someone so young.

They'd looked at me as if to say, 'What have you bought?' and I'd just looked back blankly. It was bad enough being a bridesmaid, suffering the

To the happy couple from your bridesmaid

ordeal of going through all *this* and ending up with That Man for a brother-in-law, without having it costing me money for a present as well.

'I think it's stupid,' I said, glowering at the most wonderful vase in the world. 'It won't hold hardly anything and it's too thin . . . It'll get smashed the first time you use it.' I'd tried to ping it with my fingernail, but Helen had snatched it away murmuring that she was glad *some* people were aware of the great honour given to them by being asked to be a bridesmaid, and it was a most generous and thoughtful present from an absolutely lovely little girl.

I pulled off another bit of turkey flesh and

stuffed it into my mouth. I didn't feel as if I'd had a proper meal for weeks now; I was probably losing weight at a dreadful rate and the powder blue dress would hang on me, miles too big, and I'd more than likely faint of hunger in the church.

'I might faint in the church,' I said to Mum. 'In fact I feel pretty faint now through lack of care and attention. I'm probably going to be very ill.'

'Nonsense!' Mum said. 'You look the picture of health.'

'Well, it's no thanks to you,' I said. 'I'm surprised you even remember you've got another daughter.'

'I think . . . on the whole . . . the flower arrangement,' Mum said, putting it back on. 'There! Mrs Bailey *will* be pleased.'

Helen came through to the kitchen wearing the soppy look she always wore when she'd been speaking to That Man.

'Oh, I much prefer the little bride and groom,' she said, and I groaned quietly to myself, tore off another lump of turkey and made my way out. Entering the sitting room briefly, I paused by the wedding present display, pinged the crystal vase loudly and dropped a small piece of greasy turkey skin on the card saying 'To the happy couple from your bridesmaid'.

Halfway up the stairs I heard Mum scream, 'My turkey! A cat's been at it!' but I carried on to my room regardless. All was lost, there was no way I could stop the wedding now; I just wished I could hibernate and wake up when it was all over . . .

chapter ten

'That was Helen's last night in this house!' Mum said tearfully on the wedding morning.

'Except for after the divorce,' I said, but very quietly because I wasn't much in favour.

Mum poured herself out a cup of tea and started drinking it while getting things out of the fridge, ticking things off a list, pinning her hair back, washing up saucepans and counting glasses. She consulted the list and then turned her attention on me. 'Now, Felicity will be dropped off here soon . . . but you two needn't start getting dressed for a couple of hours yet. When Dad gets back from the off-licence he'll take you to get the flowers and then later on someone will come up to your room and help you get ready.'

'I can get myself ready.'

'You heard what I said . . .' Mum said warningly. 'You do *exactly* what I say today. And don't you dare go near that cake.'

'I wasn't going to,' I said moodily. 'And it wasn't my fault if a piece of icing came off in my hand.'

'Your hand shouldn't have been near it.'

'It wouldn't have been if I'd been fed,' I muttered. 'And anyway, my bedroom's not big enough for me and Felicity and someone who's going to help us . . . Why can't I just get ready on my own? Felicity can go somewhere else.'

'No, she can't,' Mum said. She looked at the list thoughtfully. 'Mind you, your bedroom *is* small –

but Auntie Muriel and Uncle Brian will be in mine.'

'I always have the smallest everything,' I said plaintively.

'Not for much longer,' Mum said. 'You can move into Helen's room next week. Dad's already said he'll decorate it for you.'

I looked round at her in surprise. 'Really?!'

'Of course. There's no sense in it staying empty.'

'Great!' I said. Helen's room was *much* nicer – not only was it bigger, with fitted wardrobes with mirrors on them, but it also had loads of shelves and – best of all – a sink of its own. In spite of everything, I began to feel very slightly cheerful.

Mum looked at her watch. 'Now, Helen should be back from the hairdressers any minute – and then I've got *my* appointment. If Felicity arrives while I'm out you'll look after her, won't you?'

'Oh yes,' I said evilly. 'I'll do that all right.'

Mum disappeared under a mass of fruit tartlets and a moment later Helen arrived back from the hairdressers with two friends, wearing about six cans of hairspray between them. They pushed past me, giggling their way up the stairs to Helen's

room, and then Helen came out and handed me a tiny box.

'Katie! Your present for being a lovely bridesmaid. Which I'm sure you will be if you put your mind to it,' she said.

'Oh, you shouldn't have,' I said truthfully, not actually wanting a silver locket and chain which would make my neck go black.

'Little Felicity will be here soon . . . perhaps you'll give her this other box,' she said, and then she disappeared back to a chorus of screeches from within.

I looked in my box, though Mum had already told me what I'd got, and then I looked in Felicity's box to make sure she hadn't got anything better. I was reluctantly wondering whether I ought to have a bath before everyone arrived, when Mum shouted from downstairs that she wanted me.

I went down and she led me into the sitting room where there was a large cardboard box. 'I don't think you deserve this, actually,' she said, 'but Christopher insisted you should be given it.'

'What – a cardboard box?'

'Look in it,' she said.

I looked. It was a DVD player, black and silver, very modern.

'It's Christopher's old one – he brought it round for you last night. He and Helen will have her DVD player in their flat and they won't want two. Christopher said to tell you it's a proper bridesmaid's present from him.'

'Oh wow!' I said, almost lost for speech and feeling really quite cheerful altogether. I'd wanted a DVD player for ages.

'Yes, I should jolly well think it is *wow*,' said

Mum. 'And I hope you'll be a lot nicer to him from now on.'

'I will . . .' I said fervently. Maybe I'd under-estimated him . . . Maybe he was going to be OK . . . Maybe I'd be able to forgive the horrible shirts and old-fashioned trousers. Well, anyone who gave away DVD players had to be all right really.

I suppose the *really* most surprising thing that day was Felicity. She was dropped off by her mum about eleven o'clock with all her stuff, and we stood on the doorstep staring at each other. Her blonde curls were scraped back in a pony-tail and she was wearing a tracksuit which could have been the twin of mine, except that it was pale green – or had been once. Straight away I knew that she wasn't going to be goody-goody bridesmaid of the year and started to feel very cheerful indeed.

'Hello, Felicity,' I said. 'Are you coming in?'

'I hate the name Felicity,' she said. 'It's so twee. You can call me Flicka if you like.'

She followed me in, carrying her wrapped-up bridesmaid's dress and a load of other bits, and we went upstairs, past the present display in the sitting room. She pulled a face at her vase and said, 'Isn't it grrr-*ooss* . . . Mum made me buy it.'

'Absolutely gross,' I agreed, and we grinned at each other. We went upstairs, Helen came out with a blue garter on each leg to say hello and then we went into my room and plonked down on the bed.

'Guess *what*!' Flicka said. 'Dad and I just called in to wish Christopher luck and honestly, you should see what my Auntie Beattie Bailey is wearing! I nearly had hysterics on the spot!'

'What's it like?' I asked eagerly.

'Well, apparently it's the hit of the year in

Continental Cruise Wear — some sort of vast pink tent made out of nylon fluffy stuff. She looks like an elephant in candy floss! Grrr-*ooss*!'

We rolled on to my bed, giggling, and then realised we were rolling on Flicka's bridesmaid's dress and hastily hung it up.

There was just one other small surprise to come. Very small.

'I hope we haven't rolled on Mickey . . .' Flicka said anxiously, pulling out a small white handbag from under her.

'Who's Mickey?' I asked.

'A mouse,' she said apologetically. 'I know it's a corny name but my little sister wanted him to be called that.'

She dug into her bag, pulled him out and he sat on her hand and looked at us, twitching his whiskers.

'He's lovely,' I said, 'but what's he coming to the wedding for?'

'Well, because I couldn't leave him at home,' she said, 'and because . . . well . . . Auntie Beattie Bailey *hates* mice. Didn't you know?'

I shook my head.

'I thought maybe if it gets boring later on, you know . . .' she said thoughtfully.

I grinned at her. 'I think it might,' I said. And I also thought to myself that I might have been wrong all along about weddings . . .

Find out how the BIG DAY goes in

THE REVOLTING
WEDDING

MARY HOOPER

AVAILABLE NOW

Turn the page for a sneak preview . . .

BLOOMSBURY

chapter one

'When do we have to put them on?' Flicka asked, jabbing a finger towards the whisper blue brides-maids' dresses hanging on my wardrobe door. She poked at a bit of exquisite beading. 'Have you ever *seen* anything so revolting?'

I shook my head. 'Never.'

'I mean, she couldn't have found anything more gross if she'd tried.'

I shot a look at the dresses, hanging there in all their frilliness and soppiness. 'I expect she *did* try. She probably went to the Brides' Boutique place and said that none of the dresses were *quite* revolting enough so . . .'

'. . . could they kindly do her something that was *considerably* more awful,' Flicka finished in Mrs Bayleaf's voice.

I grinned. Mrs Bayleaf's real name was Mrs Bailey and she was Flicka's aunt. She was also the mother of a man called Christopher, and my sister Helen was marrying this Christopher at three o'clock – in spite of all my efforts to get her to change her mind.

As we stood glowering at the dresses there was a ring at the doorbell. 'That's Mum back from the hairdressers, I expect,' I said. 'Coming down?'

She nodded and we raced and scrambled to get out of the bedroom door first. I generously let her win, not just because Mum had told me to be nice to her, but because she – Flicka – was much better than I'd thought she was going to be. Well, Mrs

Bayleaf had described her as a delightful blond-haired little angel, so I was expecting someone foul, but now that I'd met her it was all right.

I slid down the bannisters and Flicka went down head first, slithering and sliding like an eel. We arrived at the bottom at the same time and I forward-rolled on to the *Welcome* mat and flung the door open.

It wasn't Mum, though . . .